JUST ME AND MY PUPPY

BY
MERCER MAYER

 A GOLDEN BOOK • NEW YORK

Golden Books Publishing Company, Inc., New York, New York 10106

ISBN: 0-307-59759-8   MCMXCIX
11 10 9 8 7 6

Weekly Reader is a registered trademark of the Weekly Reader Corporation.
2003 Edition

I wanted a puppy, just for me.
So I traded my baseball mitt for one.

My baby sister liked him
right away.

And, boy, were Mom and Dad surprised!
They said I could keep him if I took
care of him myself.

So I am taking very good care
of my puppy.
I feed him in the morning.

He eats every bite.

Then I put on his leash and
we go for a walk.

I am teaching my puppy
how to heel.

He is learning how to stay . . .

... except when he sees a cat.

My puppy knows lots of tricks . . .

how to sit . . .

how to play dead . . .

. and how to roll over.

He still needs some practice.

But he already knows how to fetch.

My puppy is a big help around the house.

He's a good guard dog.

He brings in
the paper
for my dad.

And he keeps me company
while I do my homework.

Sometimes my puppy
gets dirty.

Then I give him a bath.

I get him nice and dry
so he won't catch a cold.

Then we get ready for bed . . .

. . . just me and my puppy.